I0822689

Being a Black Belt is not easy. You have to train extra hard and you live by a certain code. A code that includes respect, always tell the truth, help others if they need it and be humble not bossy!

Being a Black Belt also means that I know how to protect myself and others against Bullies which is why I wanted to train in Martial Arts to begin with. And dealing with a Bully is something I know all too well!

My Bully problem began on a school day, Monday to be exact and it just so happened to be a day right after the weekend I earned my Black Belt! Abbey and I were at the bus stop waiting for the school bus to arrive chatting about my Black Belt test and how hard it was to finish it.

I was showing some bruises on my arm I had gotten on my Black Belt test to Abbey when the bus pulled up and opened its doors. "After you Abbey!" I said as I lowered my shirt sleeve and grabbed my back pack. I followed Abbey up the stairs on the bus, saying hello to our bus driver, Mr. Richard.

Mr. Richard waved hello and I turned to sit down next to Abbey. As I went to the seat Abbey was sitting in, I noticed a new girl on the bus in the back with a red shirt on looking out the window. Abbey waved to me to sit next to her and as I sat down I couldn't help but stare at the new girl.

“Do you know who that girl is sitting in the back?” I asked Abbey. Abbey turned to look at her and said “Oh that’s Beth. Her family just moved here.” Abbey moved in closer to me whispering “She doesn’t seem friendly. She ignored me when I came on the bus and said hello.” I looked back over to Beth and saw her staring right at me. She had this icy stare as if she was squinting in the sun. I quickly turned back around and sat quietly waiting to get to school.

When the bus arrived at school, Beth slowly got up out of her seat. She was HUGE! She was super tall with big hands and feet! Her clothes looked dirty and her shoes were untied. Beth began to walk past us pausing for a moment as if she had dropped something. I could see Abbey was scared and I sat in my seat waiting for her to pass trying not to look at her.

Abbey went silent and we waited until every other student was off before we left the bus quickly making our way to our lockers. I was at my locker putting my coat away when I noticed in the corner of my eye, Beth walking towards me. Feeling threatened I started thinking about my Martial Art training and began preparing in case Beth tried to attack me.

However Beth walked right past me to another student on the other side of the hallway. All of a sudden Beth grabs the girls back pack and walks off! I couldn't believe what I just saw! The girl walked away sad, looking helpless against such a Big Bad Bully!

I felt relieved when I had gotten to class and saw my teacher Mrs. Johnson smiling at me. "Hello Emma!" she said. "Please take your seats now children we need to begin class." Even though I felt safe in my class room something still bothered me. I was distracted, finding it hard to focus as Mrs. Johnson was reviewing today's assignments. All I could think about was that girl at the lockers. I couldn't help but feel bad not helping the girl against Beth. After all I'm a Black Belt! I've been trained!

Lunch time came around and even though I was hungry, I couldn't eat. What happened at the lockers was still bothering me. "Emma what's wrong?" My friend Abbey said as she sat next to me in the lunch room. As I was about to answer her, I noticed Beth walking in the room.

I stared at her with this mean look of disgust. She totally ignored me and instead walked right up to a boy taking his lunch tray from him. The boy looked as though he was about to cry and he ran out of the lunch room.

Beth sat down and began to quickly eat what was on the tray. Angry, I got up and was about to approach Beth when Mrs. Johnson approached the table saying it was time to go. I was about to let Mrs. Johnson know what had happened but before I could, Beth had left.

Not again! I was so mad at myself for not defending that boy! Two times I had the chance to protect someone and I did nothing. Abbey touched me on the shoulder letting me know we were about to leave and as I got up I swore to myself that next time Beth would not get away with bullying. Next time I will be ready!

We had a report to do for class so Mrs. Johnson took us to the Library after lunch. The Library was full of other classes working on several projects and space was tight. My friends and I found a table near the corner of the library and sat down.

I sat in my chair surrounded by my classmates trying to do my assignment but I was just too angry! Abbey leaned over to me “Emma is there something wrong? You look mad.” I looked at Abbey’s face and could tell she was worried.

Calming myself down I said "I'm okay. I'm just dealing with some things." Abbey gave me a hug and as I started to feel relaxed, I noticed that Beth had walked in.

I stared at Beth as she made her way over to the side of the Library that has a bunch of books on American History. My friend Jacob was standing over there writing down some things when Beth approached him, taking his paper.

“That’s it!” I shouted! Everyone turned and looked at me. I rushed over to Beth and snatched the paper back pushing her away from Jacob. “You may have gotten away with bullying those other kids but not this time!” I stood there, my face red with rage and my fists clenched ready to swing if Beth came at me.

“Emma what are you doing?” Mrs. Johnson shouted! I looked up at Mrs. Johnson and frantically explained what Beth had done today and how she has been bullying several kids. I shared the story of the girl at the locker having her book bag taken and the boy at lunch having his food snatched from him! And now Beth has just snatched Jacob’s paper right out of his hands!

“Mrs. Johnson, Emma is mistaken!” A voice rang from the group of kids who had surrounded me, Beth and Mrs. Johnson. The girl from the lockers emerged from the group. ‘I gave her my bag because she didn’t have one. I felt bad that her parents could not afford one for her so I gave her mine.” I turned to Beth with this puzzled look on my face.

"Mrs. Johnson, Beth didn't steal my lunch!" The boy from the lunch room came from the crowd explaining that he had given Beth his lunch. He explained that he wasn't very hungry and instead wanted to get to the library early to start working on his assignment.

Frantically I turned to Jacob. "Well what about Jacob? I saw Beth take his paper!" Jacob walked over to Mrs. Johnson. "Mrs. Johnson Beth asked me to help her find a few books to help her with her assignment because she is in need of glasses and has a hard time reading the small print on the book covers.

All of a sudden I had this gigantic pit in my stomach. I felt horrible ... I looked at Beth and began to cry asking her to forgive me for accusing her of all the horrible stuff I claimed she had done.

I couldn't look at her. Mrs. Johnson took her and me aside and had the rest of the kids sit down and continue with their assignments. "Emma? I hope this has been a valuable lesson for you. It's better to find out facts before you start assuming things. It will spare hurting someone's feelings for no reason."

With a tearful eye, I slowly looked up at Beth "I am really sorry Beth. Can you forgive me?" Beth looked at me. She didn't say anything but merely put her hand on my shoulder and while nodding her head yes, she smiled.

While I thought I was trying to protect people from a bully, I ended up becoming one myself for a brief moment forgetting how I was trained and letting my ego get the best of me! I'm happy to say Beth and I are good friends so I guess even sad stories have a happy ending! My name is Emma and I thank you for listening.

www.ingramcontent.com/pod-product-compliance
Lightning Source LLC
Chambersburg PA
CBHW080810020826
48982CB00018B/1017

* 9 7 8 0 9 8 8 7 4 6 3 2 9 *